Lakota

Lakota

Written by Maura Campbell

Story by Lance Osadchey

Lance23455@gmail.com

Lakota played by Abby

Maura Campbell
233 Crescent Road, Burlington VT
802.578.4857; ibsen3000@yahoo.com

Sequencing and Consistency Editor
Tanya Osadchey-Brown

authorHOUSE®

AuthorHouse™
1663 Liberty Drive
Bloomington, IN 47403
www.authorhouse.com
Phone: 1-800-839-8640

Published by AuthorHouse   06/12/2013

ISBN: 978-1-4817-6225-0 (sc)
ISBN: 978-1-4817-6226-7 (e)

Library of Congress Control Number: 2013910544

Written by Maura Campbell
233 Crescent Road, Burlington VT
802.578.4857; ibsen3000@yahoo.com

Sequencing and Consistency Editor
Tanya Osadchey-Brown

At present there is a song created for Lakota. It is during the transition After Darien and Lakota die.

To listen to this song go to this web page

If there are more songs they will be linked to this same page

http://www.lanceosadchey.com/FreeMusic.htm

This song was created by

Randy Smith (https://www.facebook.com/RandySmithMusic?fref=t0073),

Curt Busse (https://www.facebook.com/curt.busse.1?fref=ts),

Gary Spaulding (https://www.facebook.com/garyspaulding?fref=ts),

And Andre Maquera (https://www.facebook.com/andre.maquera?fref=ts)

Maura Campbell is an award-winning playwright whose work has been produced regionally and abroad. She has written more than thirty plays including Flower Duet, Wild Geese, Self Evidence, and Dreamtime. Campbell's plays are published by youthPlays, Independentplay(w) rights, and Smith & Kraus. Future productions include the west coast premier of Flower Duet and the premier of a commissioned play for the Full Circle Festival in April 2014. She holds an MFA in Playwriting from Hollins University.

FADE IN:

EXT. A REGAL COUNTRY HOME—UPSTATE NEW YORK—PRESENT

We see a beautiful three story brick home, beautifully manicured lawns and wide expanses of field behind it. Beyond that are mountains.

> MAN (V.O.)
>
> *Legend says that long ago, two young men were out hunting when from out of nowhere came a beautiful maiden dressed in white buckskin. One of the hunters looked upon her and, recognizing her as a sacred being, lowered his eyes. The second hunter approached her with lust in his eyes. The beautiful woman beckoned the lustful warrior to her, and as he approached a cloud of dust arose around them. When it settled, nothing but a pile of bones lay next to her. As she walked toward the respectful young hunter, she explained to him that she had merely fulfilled the other man's desire, allowing him, within that brief moment, to live a lifetime, die and decay.*

In the field we see the image of a WHITE BUFFALO. We get closer until we are seeing into its beautiful brown eyes.

CUT TO:

INT. BEDROOM—MORNING

A large bedroom, the furnishings are dark and masculine giving it an almost claustrophobic atmosphere. Huge clouds of cigarette smoke billow in the bedroom's air.

DARIEN, a woman in her thirties, but ageless, her long fingers fasten a CAMEO NECKLACE. She looks at herself in the mirror, her eyes searching for something of significance.

For a fleeting moment in the mirror's reflection she can see her HUSBAND walking from the bathroom to the stairs and the SOUND OF HIS VOICE.

> EDGAR(O.C.)
>
> Seven forty-five.

Darien's bright eyes register the intrusion of her husband, then she turns and walks out of the bedroom and down the hall. Stopping briefly, she opens the hallway window half way to let some fresh air in.

INT. KITCHEN

Edgar has finished his eggs and noisily finishes the rest of his coffee. He pulls out a GOLD POCKET WATCH from his breast pocket. He can see the reflection of his fifty-five year old face in the watch's face.

> EDGAR
>
> Eight-fifteen.

Darien looks at the wall clock in the kitchen.

> DARIEN
>
> Eight-seventeen.

He squints at the clock.

EDGAR

My grandfather gave me this watch.

For emphasis, he pats the breast of his thousand dollar suit.

DARIEN

I know.

EDGAR

It's a hundred years old.

DARIEN

I know.

EDGAR

He bought it with his first commission check. So if it says eight fifteen, in my book that's what time it is.

He gets up abruptly leaving his dishes on the table. Darien looks at them, and then clears his place.

INT/EXT. DOORWAY TO HOME—SOON AFTER

Edgar walks down the stone walkway to his car, igniting his 3rd cigarette of the morning. His driver stands at attention. Edgar turns to Darien who stands in the doorway.

EDGAR

Since it's your birthday, I want to take you shopping and to a fancy restaurant. Might as well have dinner at the Charboneaux. I've got tickets to . . . .

                          DARIEN
          All right, that sounds fun. I'll take the train in.

Edgar hesitates.

                          EDGAR
          You're wearing that?

Darien's hand instinctively goes to the brooch. She smiles.

                          DARIEN
          My grandmother gave me this brooch.

                          EDGAR
          I mean the whole outfit.

                          DARIEN
          What would you like me to wear?

                          EDGAR
          I don't know. Something with buttons. Put on some lipstick. It's
          a big day.

He blows Darien a kiss, then gets in the car and drives away.

She walks outside now and feels the sunshine on her face. We can see a
better view of their house, a large, brick wonder with expanses of lawn
and gardens of flowers. This is her space, the outdoors.

The wind picks up a little and blows her hair around her face. She turns on the garden hose and gently waters her flowers. She hums something, a haunting melody.

In the near distance she hears A DOG BARKING. She stands up straight and listens carefully, moving her head, making small adjustments. The sounds becomes FAINTER but in some way, it is more meaningful for her. She runs into the house leaving the hose running in the grass.

INT. DARIEN'S HOUSE

We now get a better picture of the house she lives in. The living room is formal with large framed photos of Edgar and his ancestors, large, mustached men, hunting scenes, group shots of grandfathers and uncles with politicians. He is a man's man and this house is his home.

Furniture is polished cherry and mahogany, pieces handed down but hardly used. Somewhere in this house there must be a shrine to Darien but it is not for public view.

There is a dining room, as well, large and formal, again, a room that hardly looks used. Heavy brocade drapes would keep out the sunshine, but the house faces north. One can imagine perhaps pheasant served or venison, food that the patriarch and his entourage have shot the day before and the servants have prepared.

We then turn and go up the stairs, also dark and gleaming, sixteen to the first landing, then we go up another twelve to a small attic room where we find Darien.

INT. DARIEN'S ARTISTIC ROOM

The walls of this room are PAINTED MURALS, A GODDESS is in the center and she wears a multi-colored cloak and in the folds lives children and animals and behind and above this goddess is a celestial sky.

In the three dimensional world, this goddess and this sky are finite. But look at it with another eye and it expands forever. This is how Darien sees it at this moment.

She picks up a paintbrush, yes, this is her work. And she paints the outline of a large feather and puts it in the Goddess's hand.

Then she gets up and goes to a closet. Inside are various dresses and blouses, perhaps more to her husband's liking? She selects a red silk blouse and gray skirt, takes off her brooch, and changes into them.

The colors suit her. Darien is beautiful. She finds a ribbon and creates a necklace for the brooch and hangs it around her neck. Then she opens a drawer and takes out a small felt hat with a beautiful feather and walks out of the room.

The scene moves to and lingers on the photo album. It is a picture of an OLDER WOMAN; she looks very much like Darien but from another time. Her dark hair is plaited. She wears the same CAMEO NECKLACE.

INT. SUBWAY—A FEW HOURS LATER

Outside a thunderstorm is forming. Darien sits on the subway. It's the usual assortment of fellow passengers, truant kids with IPODs, elderly

women with packages, business men with shiny shoes. The train rumbles and jerks.

There are two thugs in the train car with her. There are a few other people. One of the thugs has a scar on his right cheek. The other has a snake tattoo on his arm. Both are of medium height and muscular. Wearing thug clothes T-shirts. They are glancing at her giving her winks and nods and smiling trying to get her attention. She does notice them but ignores them.

THUG ONE

You want company?

Darien glances up at him.

DARIEN

No! Get lost!

He smiles and sits down beside her and makes pick-up talk. She ignores him.

Suddenly a MUSICIAN/PAN HANDLER comes up the aisle. He is African American, a Mr. Bojangles, with a homemade guitar. He sings.

MR. BOJANGLES

(sings)

Darien is the only one who watches him. The businessmen read their newspapers, the kids are lost in their own musical worlds, plugged into their IPODS. One or two older women throw a few coins in his tip can but only Darien seems to enjoy his singing.

He looks at her. He winks and continues strumming.

As she listens, behind her, the city landscape rushing past becomes a wilderness and something, or someone, seems to be running through the woods as fast as the train.

Darien senses its presence and she turns to look but it is now the station and the train slows down.

INT./EXT. TRAIN PLATFORM

Darien is looking through the train doors as they close on Mr. Bojangles. She has stuffed his tip can with twenty dollar bills.

EXT. 8TH AVENUE NEW YORK CITY

Outside Penn Station, the world has arrived, tourists, taxis, the rush of humanity on the road to nowhere.

Darien stands on the street.

> VOICE (O.C.)
> Missy, hey you missy, you taxi?

Darien sees a man in a taxi. He has rolled down the window and leaned over. Dark hair in a pony tail, Indian. Eastern Indian.

> INDIAN TAXI DRIVER
> You taxi?

Darien gets in and the taxi speeds off in a blaze of smoke. The smoke takes shape in a vaguely human form and follows the taxi.

FADE OUT.

EXT. 78 WALL STREET, HUSBAND'S OFFICE—SOON AFTER

The exterior of the building is cold and grey. In GOLD LETTERS A SIGN READS: BAER AND SONS FINANCIAL SERVICES. A DOORMAN, resplendent in his uniform opens the door for Darien and she enters. A gush of wind enters behind her and a single feather floats just behind her head.

INT. LOBBY

A magnificent chandelier looms over the polished marble floor. Its glittering light sprays light as Darien walks toward the gleaming elevator. It opens. TWO BUSINESSMEN in black suits stand at attention. Darien steps inside.

ONE BUSINESSMAN

Going up?

The doors close. We see a back view of the men and Darien. Underneath of the men's hats, we get a glimpse of his shaved head and a bit of tattooed letters. This is not your average businessman. Nor is his friend.

INT. BAER AND SONS OFFICES

Darien stands in front of a medium sized mahogany desk with a plaque that reads, RECEPTIONIST. The RECEPTIONIST looks up at Darien and smiles a perfect smile.

17

RECEPTIONIST

Big day, huh? Get yourself some ice tea over there, It's really good.

Darien goes to the alcove and with her back to the secretary pours herself a large glass of ice tea and gulps it down rapidly, then puts the glass down, very gently.

DARIEN

Thanks that was just great.

Darien follows the secretary's big ass down a long, wide hallway toward a door.

INT. CONFERENCE ROOM

Edgar and his son, PHILLIP, SEVERAL HARD BOILED EXECUTIVES and their WASPY WIVES, and a MAN WITH A PONY TAIL stand around a big table with a MAGNIFICENT CAKE surrounded by appetizers and bottles of champagne. The cake reads, CONGRATULATIONS SON.

Phillip comes forward to greet Darien, his perfectly manicured hand takes hers and he kisses her a little loudly on the cheek. He smiles at her. His once handsome face is a bit bloated but every hair on his head is in place.

PHILLIP

So glad you could share this day with us, Darien. His face DISTORTS GROTESQUELY for a nano-second and then returns to normal.

PHILLIP (CONT'D)
(to the crowd)
You all know my father's wife.

EDGAR
Someone get her a glass of champagne!

The pony tailed man is at Darien's side. He hands her a glass.

EDGAR (CONT'D)
I think everyone is here? Well, well, well, I hope nobody here takes this as a sign of my getting old, rather that my son has at last . . . matured.

Appreciative chuckles all around. Phillip smiles broadly, except for his eyes then his face hardens but the smile remains.

EDGAR (CONT'D)
We had disagreements and I said and did things that, well, I profoundly regret. And I apologize. I ask your forgiveness.

Edgar signs documents that make Phillip a full partner. Phillip goes to his father and they embrace. A tear falls from his eye. But Darien is seeing Phillips reflection in the window behind him.

CUT TO:

INT. JEWELRY STORE, 5TH AVENUE—LATER

Edgar and Darien are looking at displays of colorful gemstones set in necklaces, bracelets and rings. A SALESLADY, young with very dark hair wearing TURQUOISE JEWELRY smiles at them.

> SALESLADY
>
> Can I show you something?

Darien looks at one of the Saleslady's rings, a large piece of turquoise set in silver.

> DARIEN
>
> This is most unusual.

> SALESLADY
>
> Oh yes. But you won't find anything like it here.

> DARIEN
>
> A gift?

The Saleslady smiles.

> SALESLADY
>
> Isn't everything?

EXT. THE STREET

Edgar and Darien hail a taxi.

EDGAR

There's a store near the restaurant that sells imported furniture.

They get in the taxi.

INT. FURNITURE STORE

Edgar and Darien look through the ornate Mediterranean furniture. Darien pauses to admire a beautiful table.

EDGAR

Would you like that?

Darien seems surprised.

DARIEN

What? Oh, no, I just like looking at it.

Edgar frowns a little bit.

EDGAR

In the two years we've been married, you have hardly ever let me buy you a gift.

He takes her hand and looks deeply into her eyes.

EDGAR (CONT'D)

Why is that?

                         DARIEN

Seeing these beautiful things with you is enough to satisfy me.

Darien chooses her next words carefully.

                         DARIEN

If you never accept a gift from someone, it can never be taken

from you.

He shakes his head at his beautiful wife, but smiles.

                         EDGAR

Can I at least buy you dinner?

Darien turns her head in the direction of the street.

                         DARIEN

Mm, can you smell that?

Now she smiles.

                      DARIEN (CONT'D)

Steak!

She pauses and considers.

                      DARIEN(CONT'D)

And I smell roses. Roses on the tables.

They walk outside.

EXT. THE STREET

Darien looks up at the sky. Storm clouds gather.

INT. THE RESTAURANT

Edgar and Darien are being seated at a table next to a window overlooking a river. On the table is a small vase of roses. The MAITRE 'D holds out Darien's chair and places menus in front of them.

> MAITRE 'D
> So wonderful to see you again, sir. And your lovely wife.

Edgar smiles at Darien and opens the wine list.

LATER

The WAITER puts dinner plates in front of EDGAR and Darien. They have both ordered steak béarnaise with baked potatoes, green beans and salad.

Darien cuts into her steak. It is very, very rare and blood rushes out. Edgar raises his eyebrows at the sight.

> DARIEN
> It's how I like it.

She puts a bloody piece of steak in her mouth and chews.

INT. LINCOLN CENTER—LATER

Edgar and Darien watch as TONY dies in MARIA'S arms in West Side Story.

EXT. THE STREET—AFTER THE SHOW

Edgar and Darien are among the throngs of theater goers who spill into the street. Now a light unpleasant rain starts.

> EDGAR
> We can pick up the Metro over on 72nd.

Darien and Edgar cross the busy two lanes in front of Lincoln Center.

They start down Broadway and Darien notices a BLACK LABRADOR RETRIEVER huddled in the shadows of the darkened alley, next to some garbage cans. The dog looks intently at Darien as if she is trying to communicate something. Darien instinctively puts her hand to her neck and her Cameo necklace.

From the alley TWO THUGS emerge. The street is suddenly and inexplicably deserted.

> FIRST THUG
> Little late for you to be out, isn't it? Hey I know you.

At that moment Darien senses the THUGS want more than to rob them.

EDGAR

We're just catching our train—

Edgar tries to push through the two thugs but they block his way. One thug takes out a SWITCHBLADE.

SECOND THUG

What you got in your pockets?

Edgar immediately takes out his wallet.

EDGAR

You can have it. There's a couple hundred dollars. Take it.

Darien narrows her eyes.

FIRST THUG

Let's have that purse.

He jerks it out of Darien's hands. The Second Thug frisks Edgar. He finds his GOLD WATCH and holds it up to admire.

SECOND THUG

I always wanted one of these.

Then he looks at Darien's Cameo.

SECOND THUG (CONT'D)

Okay. Gimme.

Darien touches the Cameo protectively. She smiles.

DARIEN

My grandmother gave this to me. She'd rather you didn't have it.

The First Thug is tickled by this.

FIRST THUG

Oh, she'd rather, would she?

The thug looks menacingly at her and steps towards her. His eyes dilate and beads of perspiration form on his upper lip and his lip quivers.

Before he can make his move, Darien gives the Dog a slight nod. The Dog bares her teeth and growls menacingly.

FIRST THUG (CONT'D)

What, I've got to take care of you, too?

The dog jumps at the first thug, biting him on the thigh as the thug whips the knife downward at the dog. As the knife cuts the dog on the shoulder area, Darien swings her left palm flat out into the thug's throat. He chokes and the knife flies up out of his hand as he bends forward gasping for air.

Darien jumps high and grabs the knife in midair by the handle and as she comes back to the ground brings the knife directly into the second thug's chest. She then pulls the knife out and replants it again into his chest. Blood flows and he drops dying to the ground.

The First thug has regained his breath.

FIRST THUG

You bitch! Now you die!

He rushes at Darien but she nimbly steps aside and he flies past her. Now both face each other and Darien rushes at him. She jumps to the side and makes four five passes like this, avoiding the angry thug. She kicks him in the leg and mid body 4 or 5 times. He gets very confused and tired and falls to the ground. Darien continues her onslaught, jumping over the thug and kicking him time and time again. Her voice is filling the alley.

On her close pass the thug manages to grab her leg and brings her to the ground. Both are fighting for their lives. Darien's blouse gets ripped open and her skirt pushed to her thigh. First she is winning, then the thug. In a roll over maneuver, Darien winds up holding the thugs neck in her arm with a choke hold. She struggles to keep her arm in the position and eventually the thug passes out, but Darien keeps her grip and the thug dies.

EDGAR
What did you . . . where did you . . . ?

DARIEN
They got what they deserved. No one will miss them.

Edgar is still holding his chest and breathing rapidly. Darien swiftly goes about retrieving Edgar's wallet. She looks for the watch and cannot find it.

EDGAR

Come on, let's get out of here.

Darien looks at the Dog. She lies on her side; her coat is wet with blood.

DARIEN

We're taking the dog.

Edgar looks around frantically.

DARIEN(CONT.)

I said we're taking the dog.

Darien sees a taxi cab. She picks up the dog.

DARIEN (CONT'D)

Taxi!

The taxi pulls up to the curb. Darien and Edgar get in with the dog. We see the taxi driver's profile. It is the same taxi driver that picked up Darien when she arrived in the city.

EXT. GREENWICH ANIMAL HOSPITAL

The taxi pulls up. Darien and Edgar get out with the dog.

He leans into the taxi.

EDGAR

How much do I—

But the taxi speeds off.

INT. ANIMAL HOSPITAL EXAM ROOM

An ELDERLY FEMALE DOCTOR, with long with braids and piercing blue eyes, examines the dog.

DOCTOR

Ah, yes, I know, it hurts. Your owners let this happen to you?

She shaves the area where the dog has been cut and applies antiseptic. The dog cries in pain.

DOCTOR (CONT'D)

Yes, but it's good for you. Hopefully they learn a lesson at your expense.

Now she wraps the dog's wound with gauze

DOCTOR (CONT'D)

I'll give you some antibiotics. She'll need to take them for ten days. She shouldn't move very much. You'll have to carry her outside to do her business.

Darien strokes the dog's head. They look at each other, a bond. The dog gently licks Darien's hand.

DOCTOR

And how are you folks going to take care of this?

A credit card is produced from a stained wallet. When the Doctor sees the name her attitude dramatically changes 180 degrees.

DOCTOR (CONT'D)

She has a great spirit. She will be great. Call me at any time. The stitches are self dissolving.

Hmmm a friend, Lakota. And an Indian name at that. It means friend, like an ally.

CUT TO:

OUTSIDE THE ANIMAL HOSPITAL

Darien, Edgar and the dog get back inside the taxi. The doctor watches from the window. The doctor's face squints through the glass as she watches the taxi pull away. Behind her the scene morphs into the plains of North Dakota. She is on a horse and she rides away.

FADE OUT.

INT. EDGAR AND DARIEN'S HOME—THE NEXT MORNING

Edgar is asleep in bed. Lakota, yes, Darien has officially named her. Lakota is on a makeshift dog bed in one corner of the room. Her eyes are on the bedroom door. THE SOUND OF WATER RUNNING can be heard then it stops. Darien enters the bedroom.

Lakota is instantly more alert but has to struggle to stand. Darien comes over to her and kneels down.

> DARIEN
>
> There, there.

A deep understanding has already developed between Darien and Lakota. Darien puts her hand lightly on Lakota's bandage and rests it for a moment.

CUT TO:

LAKOTA'S PERSPECTIVE

The place where Darien touched Lakota now glows faintly.

BACK TO:

DARIEN AND EDGAR

Edgar's eyes are open. One side of his face is slack.

> DARIEN
>
> Edgar?

She touches his face. He moans softly.

EXT. EDGAR AND DARIEN'S HOME—SOON AFTER

EMT'S carry Edgar on a stretcher to an ambulance. Darien follows them; she is wrapped in a long, wool shawl. Lakota is by her side.

INT. HOSPITAL CORRIDOR—LATER

Darien walks down a hallway. It is white and gleaming. She has braided her long hair and wears the feather in it.

CUT TO:

INT. EDGAR AND DARIEN'S HOME

Lakota is in the entry, her eyes on the door. THE DOORBELL RINGS. Lakota stands up with difficulty. It RINGS AGAIN. She begins to growl. Again, IT RINGS. Lakota barks and barks; it is clear she does not trust whoever is on the other side of that door.

CUT TO:

INT. INTENSIVE CARE UNIT

Edgar is hooked up to various lifesaving tubes and monitors. A technician reads his vital signs. He is asleep for now and calm. Darien sits at his bedside and holds his hand. Then he opens his eyes and looks at his wife. He smiles.

EDGAR
I never bought you that gift.

DARIEN

And yet you gave me everything.

He closes his eyes and his face relaxes. He understands. And so Darien closes her eyes, too, perhaps in prayer. Her skin begins to glow faintly as she does this, then she is suddenly jolted back.

PHILLIP (O.C.)

How is he?

CUT TO:

LAKOTA BARKING

BACK TO:

DARIEN AND PHILLIP

Darien turns to see her stepson. He is smiling kindly but his face is dotted with perspiration.

DARIEN

Asleep for now.

PHILLIP

Heart attack?

The Son notices the feather in her hair. He takes it out.

A VOICE

Mrs. Baer?

Darien and Phillip turn to see DR. GONZALEZ, a big, muscular man who seems to fill up the room in size and spirit.

CUT TO:

DR. GONZALEZ'S OFFICE

Dr. Gonzalez opens the door and Phillip and Darien enter. When he closes the door, we notice a framed collection of arrowheads on the wall. He sits across from Darien and Phillip.

DR. GONZALEZ

It's called a CVA. Cerebral vascular accident.

PHILLIP

What's the prognosis?

DR. GONZALEZ

Once we stabilize him we'll be able to determine the cause. Could be thrombosis, an aneurysm.

Dr. Gonzalez looks at Darien.

DR. GONZALEZ (CONT'D)

How are you doing?

DARIEN

I'm scared.

PHILLIP

Darien, Darien, there's no need to be scared. Dad has the best care here, right?

Dr. Gonzalez nods but only looks at Darien.

PHILLIP (CONT'D)

And I'm here. For you. For whatever you need.

Phillip takes Darien's hand. The arrowheads behind him instantly come alive. They are now attached to the spears they once were part of and are aimed—all of them—at the back of Phillip's hand. Dr. Gonzalez watches this with some amusement.

DR. GONZALEZ

He's right. We're here for whatever you need.

Darien removes her hand. The arrowheads return to the case. Now the doctor looks at Phillip.

DR. GONZALEZ (CONT'D)

There is absolutely nothing to worry about. Here is my home number.

He writes it down on a piece of paper and gives it to Darien.

DR. GONZALEZ (CONT'D)

In case you have questions and I'm not here.

PHILLIP
Do you give your number to everyone?

DR. GONZALEZ
Everyone I'm trying to help.

He turns back to Darien.

DR. GONZALEZ (CONT'D)
We'll know more in about twenty-four hours. You should go home, try not to worry.

Darien folds up the paper and puts it in a special compartment in her purse. She gets up, Phillip follows suit.

DARIEN
Cardiovascular—

DR. GONZALEZ
Accident.

DARIEN
There are no accidents.

Darien and Phillip leave the office. Dr. Gonzalez watches them go. But then he smiles ever so slightly.

FADE TO BLACK.

EXT. DARIEN AND EDGAR'S PROPERTY—WEEKS LATER

Lakota is running through the fields as fast as she can go, not for play, but with a desperate urgency.

CUT TO:

INT. POLICE STATION EVIDENCE ROOM

Close up of a plastic bag containing Edgar's watch. DETECTIVE BLADE signs his name on a chain of custody form and puts it in his pocket.

LEAD DETECTIVE

If you're done with fingerprints, photos, DNA and everything else you do I'll sign the pocket watch out?

EXT. EDGAR AND DARIEN'S HOUSE

A police car comes up the drive. It stops. DETECTIVE O'CONNOR and DETECTIVE BLADE get out. They look at the stately house and then at each other.

CUT TO:

LAKOTA RUNNING

BACK TO:

THE HOUSE

The Detectives knock at the door.

BACK TO:

LAKOTA RUNNING

She runs leaps and takes flight.

BACK TO:

THE HOUSE

Darien opens the door.

DARIEN

May I help you?

Detective O'Connor, tall and cuddly like a bear, smiles down at Darien. Detective Blade, the heavy, tries to look and see what might be behind Darien.

O'CONNOR

I'm Detective O'Connor, this is my partner Detective Blade. May we come in?

Darien moves outside and looks for Lakota.

DARIEN

Lakota! Lakota!

She looks around for her dog.

DARIEN (CONT'D)

I let her out for a min—here she is.

Lakota, now without a bandage, limps from behind the house up to Darien. Darien kneels and pets her dog.

DARIEN (CONT'D)

I was getting worried.

Darien turns to the policemen.

DARIEN (CONT'D)

What is this about?

O'Connor takes a deep breath.

O'CONNOR

I'd rather we talked inside.

Darien looks to Lakota for approval. Lakota provides it.

INT. EDGAR AND DARIEN'S HOUSE

The dining room furniture has been removed. EDGAR is in a hospital bed. He is awake but paralyzed on one side. Darien has filled the room with flowers and flower boxes on the windows as well as bird feeders. It is a virtual paradise. The walls have been painted as murals of water falls and fields and strong iconic animals, buffalo, deer, eagles and dogs. These creatures are active but also they watch.

> O'CONNOR
> Mr. Baer, I'm Detective O'Connor.

> DARIEN (to EDGAR)
> They want to ask us some questions.

> (to the detectives)
> Would you like to sit down?

The men sit down. Detective Blade, in spite of himself, cannot stop looking at the incredible room. Lakota sits on the threshold.

> DARIEN (CONT'D)
> Lakota, come here.

Lakota enters.

> EDGAR
> (with great difficulty)
> Lakota . . .

Lakota puts her front paws on the bed and licks his hand.

                         O'CONNOR
We're here to talk about an incident that happened about four
weeks ago.

                         DARIEN
Four weeks, four weeks. We were in the city four weeks ago. A
Friday

                         O'CONNOR
This was a Friday. The fourteenth.

Edgar looks at Darien steadily. He wants to speak but, of course, cannot.

                         BLADE
Homicide. Two men, one killed with a knife, the other . . .

Blade looks at Lakota.

                      BLADE (CONT'D)
The other strangled.

Lakota wants to play now, she finds a ball and brings it to Blade.

                         DARIEN
My goodness . . .

                         BLADE
Cut the crap, what do you know about this?

O'Connor stands up abruptly.

> O'CONNOR
>
> Hey, hey, settle down. Settle down. Why don't you go outside and take some pictures.

> BLADE
>
> I'm not stupid—

> O'CONNOR
>
> We'll need to get shots on all sides. And the car.

Blade gives Darien, Lakota and O'Connor a dirty look and leaves. As he goes, the scene on the wall follows him out the front door.

O'Connor smiles brightly at his audience, including Lakota, who appears to be sleeping. But when he looks away the dog studies him intently.

> O'CONNOR (CONT'D)
>
> We picked up a young punk about two nights ago. He was on drugs. Raving about his two friends that were killed in a subway station around 15th Street. Said a dog and a lady. And an . . . older man. In the alley way, where the two thugs were murdered, the police found this golden watch with your husband's initials on it. Is it his?

> DARIEN
>
> Yes it is. My husband told me he thought the watch had been pick-pocketed while he was on the train. I suspect that possibly

these two came about it from either one of their friends . . . or they did the pick pocketing themselves.

O'CONNOR

Could be. We discovered one of the thugs lived in a small town near your house. He could easily have stolen the watch from your husband. AND we also talked with a veterinarian in a 24-hour clinic and she said she remembered you and your husband bringing a dog in with an injury. Is that the dog in the corner of the room?

DARIEN

Yes. After the play we found the dog injured and took her to the vet's. Then we brought her home and adopted her.

O'CONNOR

Did you see anything suspicious? The murders happened near the clinic.

DARIEN

Other than the injured dog? No I didn't see anything suspicious.

O'Connor opens his hand to Edgar and reveals the watch. Edgar struggles to sit up.

DARIEN

Please, don't darling—

He struggles some more.

O'CONNOR

The punk we picked up. He had it on him. Said he ran out with it as his friends were being slaughtered. I think it's got your initials on it, sir.

The front door slams. We hear but do not see Detective Blade.

BLADE (O.C.)
We just got a report. Sargent Perry picked up a couple in Harlem, similar description with a dog. They're running DNA but I think it's going to be a fit.

O'Connor looks at Darien.

O'CONNOR
What do you know?

O'Connor looks at his partner, who enters the room.

O'CONNOR (CONT'D)
Could be a coincidence.

BLADE
I don't believe in coincidences.

O'CONNOR
Okay, well, like I said, if I have any other questions.

O'Connor walks past Blade. We see him from the back.

DARIEN

Thank you, Detective O'Connor.

The Detective does not give Darien the watch but instead puts it in his pocket. He smiles at Edgar.

O'CONNOR

Those two got want they deserved. I'd like to know the whole story one day.

Darien opens the door.

DARIEN

Who knows, perhaps one day you will.

FADE OUT.

EXT. EDGAR AND DARIEN'S HOUSE—SOME MONTHS LATER

Late in the afternoon. Autumn in its full glory.

INT. DINING ROOM

Edgar is much weaker. He is still in the dining room and the murals are somehow more somber, the colors more muted, and the creatures have their eyes on him as if waiting patiently for something to change. As if they are waiting to welcome him home.

We hear Darien and Phillip in another part of the house arguing. Edgar hears it, too but he is powerless to interfere.

PHILLIP(O.C.)

Fine, keep him at home; you think you know better than anyone else—

DARIEN (O.C.)

I know what He wants—

Phillip goes out the front door, slamming it. Darien enters the dining room and sits by Edgar's side.

DARIEN (CONT'D)

That's his way of caring for you, but I explained.

Darien looks at Edgar's face. He is terrified and desperate to tell her something.

DARIEN (CONT'D)

What is it?

He opens his good hand and shows her his imaginary gold watch. He gives it to her and she pretends to take it.

DARIEN (CONT'D)

I thought I would—

He shakes his head vigorously and she understands he wants her to keep it.

DARIEN (CONT'D)

Just until you're better.

He relaxes now. He closes his eyes. The walls of the murals come to animated life and fill the room with peace and warmth.

Lakota, too, is part of this scene, as part of the animation.

FADE TO BLACK.
FADE IN:

INT. LIVING ROOM—WEEKS LATER

Edgar sits in his recliner. Lakota lies on a sheepskin rug on the other side of the room. EDGAR is frailer, his breath is labored but his mind is still clear.

He awkwardly lights a cigarette. Lakota notices and walks out of the room.

EDGAR
Okay, okay, I'll go outside.

Edgar walks feebly to the front door and opens it. Lakota follows him outside.

EXT. THE FRONT YARD

Edgar looks around at his property. He realizes this is probably the last time he will look at it in this way, that his strength and life are fading fast.

He sits down on a porch chair. The Dog instinctively comes and sits and watches him. EDGAR coughs a few times and puts out his cigarette under his foot. He looks at the Dog.

EDGAR

Would you like to go for a ride? I'll bet you would. Maybe if I took you for a ride you'd like me better. I can't help being jealous, you know. But I know you'll look after her. Promise me. Please promise me.

Edgar waits and when he is satisfied . . .

EDGAR (CONT'D)

There is something I need to tell you. I mean, there is something I need to tell someone. A terrible, terrible confession, something so awful, the worst day of my life. I remember it so vividly and have tried too hard to put it out of my mind . . .

Edgar begins to cough again. It's as if the words are choking him. Finally, he stops.

EDGAR (CONT'D)

If I added all the horrible days I ever had and all the horrible days you ever had they couldn't come close to being as horrible as that day. Can I tell you? Can you help me?

The memory is too much for Edgar. Tears fall down his cheeks and instead of wracking coughs he is shaken with grief.

EDGAR (CONT'D)

But I know I will take these memories with me to my grave. Why can't I unburden myself. Perhaps this has been my hell. Perhaps death will really be a release.

INT. INTENSIVE CARE UNIT—Several weeks later.

Edgar is talking to a white wall as if were his Doctor.

> EDGAR
>
> No, damn it, I do not want your expensive chemotherapy. It wouldn't work any way. Look man I got lots of enjoyment and that's it. We all die. I knew the facts and decided on continuing—so get lost. Can't I make a personal choice without the holy approval of you white coats. What do you really care?

Darien sits by his side on his hospital bed and Lakota sits with her. Edgar is very close to death.

A YOUNG WOMAN enters, a social worker. Her name tag reads "HOLLY HOWARD." She is a blonde bundle of bad news.

> HOLLY
>
> Mrs. Baer?

Darien looks up at Holly's smiling face.

> DARIEN
>
> Yes?

> HOLLY
>
> I wonder if we can—

She gestures that they leave the room and talk. Then she speaks loudly.

HOLLY (CONT'D)

HOW ARE YOU? I'M JUST GOING TO STEAL YOUR PRETTY WIFE
FOR A MOMENT.

She motions to Darien.

HOLLY (CONT'D)

Shall we?

INT. HOLLY HOWARD'S OFFICE

Holly's office walls are filled with framed posters with inspirational
pictures and slogans "HAPPINESS IS A CHOICE," and others the same.
The walls are painted yellow, like her hair. What we really notice are her
sharp little teeth. Darien sits next to her desk.

HOLLY

So, you know, I like to have a chance to talk to all the patients'
families. As I can.

DARIEN

Funny, we didn't talk when he was admitted last June.

HOLLY

Oh, no, no, I only talk to families without insurance.

Darien looks at Holly's brightly smiling face.

DARIEN

Excuse me?

HOLLY

You're insurance, well, your husband's insurance lapsed. The—

She looks in a file.

HOLLY (CONT'D)

Yes, the fifteenth, today is the twenty-second.

DARIEN

That's impossible.

HOLLY

No, we checked. Well, double-checked. It was . . . here it is . . . cancelled.

Darien's stares and thinks.

DARIEN

By my husband's son . . .

HOLLY

Yes, we tried to get in touch with him. We got a message through his secretary, let's see where, yes, he says he's not responsible for his father, to get in touch with you.

Darien gets up.

DARIEN

I have to go, if you'll excuse me—

HOLLY

We're just wondering.

Darien looks at her another time. The bright sunny smile has returned.

HOLLY (CONT'D)

How much money do you have in your checking account?

CUT TO:

EXT. BAER AND BAER'S OFFICES

Darien gets out of a taxi with Lakota. The DOORMAN opens the door; he looks very much like the guy we met on the subway, in fact, as she goes in he sings:

CUT TO:

INT. BAER AND BAER'S OFFICES

Darien rushes by the receptionist.

CYNTHIA

Mrs. Baer, you can't go in there and that dog—

But Darien and Lakota go in anyway.

INT. PHILLIP'S OFFICE

Phillip is on the phone. He looks out a large plate glass window. In its reflection he sees the entire Lakota Nation. But when he turns around it is just Darien and Lakota.

PHILLIP

So.

Cynthia stands in the doorway behind Darien.

PHILLIP (CONT'D)
(to Cynthia)

It's all right.

Cynthia retreats. Lakota gives her a warning look.

PHILLIP (CONT'D)

Sit down, sit down, I've been meaning to call.

DARIEN

How could you do this to your father?

PHILLIP

How could I do what?

DARIEN

You've cancelled our insurance—

89

PHILLIP

Oh—

Phillip gets up and comes to the other side of the desk. He leans against it, close to Darien.

PHILLIP (CONT'D)

When my father made me a full partner he included a rights of survivorship clause—

DARIEN

He's not dead yet!

PHILLIP

Once he went on life support, the clause went into effect.

DARIEN

I'm going to—

PHILLIP

What, sue me? You haven't got any money.

Darien looks, for the very first time, afraid.

PHILLIP (CONT'D)

Go ahead. Check.

Phillip's phone rings. He picks it up.

PHILLIP (CONT'D)

Hello? . . . Yes . . . yes . . . I see . . . no, thank you, I'll let her know . . . I appreciate it . . . yes, it's probably for the best . . . my thanks again.

He turns to Darien.

PHILLIP (CONT'D)

I'm so sorry. My father has died.

CUT TO:

INT/EXT. THE STREET OUTSIDE BAER AND BAER'S OFFICES

Darien and Lakota run outside. Darien looks inside her wallet for cash. She has two twenty dollar bills. She looks at her credit cards and fears for the worst. She looks at Lakota.

DARIEN

Lakota—

A taxi pulls up and a door opens. Lakota jumps inside. The Taxi Driver rolls down the window. We have seen him before. He brought Darien to this building in June. He smiles. Darien gets inside.

The Doorman closes the door. The two men nod to each other. The taxi drives away. The Doorman whistles that tune.

FADE TO BLACK.

EXT. HILLSIDE GRAVEYARD

Darien, Phillip, his WIFE, and their YOUNG SON are among the mourners. His casket is in a dug grave.

The Wife's sleek blonde hair looks luminous underneath a black veiled hat. Phillip's son, a frail looking four year old, stands between his parents. His eyes follow a BLUEBIRD that is perched on a nearby monument.

Darien looks lost among Edgar's family and colleagues. Several feet behind her and watching closely is Lakota.

A MINISTER addresses the mourners.

> MINISTER
> Lo! I tell you a mystery. We shall not all sleep, but we shall all be changed, in a moment, in the twinkling of an eye, at the last trumpet. For the trumpet will sound, and the dead will be raised imperishable, and we shall be changed. For this perishable nature must put on the imperishable, and this mortal nature must put on immortality.

The Young Son watches Darien. He smiles.

FADE OUT.

EXT. EDGAR AND DARIEN'S HOUSE—NIGHT

The sky is brilliantly lit with stars, constellations are swirling. It is as if Vincent van Gogh has painted this sky.

We get closer to the house and notice a pair of giant wings only partially seen above the roof. Then they rise above the roof. But they are not the wings of an angel; they are the wings of PEGASUS.

INT. EDGAR AND DARIEN'S HOUSE

Darien has packed what she wants and the boxes and suitcases are in the front hallway. We can faintly hear the SOUND OF A WOMAN SINGING. We move into the living room. The SOUND is louder but we notice that the stereo system is off. But behind this room separated by French doors, is a second living room. There is the Woman that Darien saw in her husband's office. She is singing to a GROUP, accompanied by a MAN playing a piano. Among the group is a much younger EDGAR. But we understand that this is a vision of something that happened long ago.

Darien comes down the stairs with Lakota. She hears the music and walks through the first living room.

He turns and looks at Darien. He gets up and walks toward her. His body is transparent but still vibrant. He takes something imaginary out of his pocket and gives it to her. It is his grandfather's POCKET WATCH.

Darien picks up a suitcase and goes out the door into the night. Lakota looks at EDRAR and then follows DARIEN. We still hear the SOUND OF SINGING but it begins to grow louder and louder, now not one voice but many, a CHOIR OF ANGELS SING.

EXT. EDGAR AND DARIEN'S HOUSE

Darien gets into a car with Lakota. As she drives away we notice a FOR SALE SIGN at the end of the driveway.

As the car pulls away, we have the feeling we are following her, as if we are riding on the back of a large animal, running.

Lakota looks through the car window as they go faster and faster and we hear the same Man's Voice we heard in the beginning of the story.

                    MAN (V.O.)
White Buffalo Calf Woman instructed the young man to go back to the People and tell them to prepare for her arrival to teach them of the way to pray. The young hunter obeyed. When White Buffalo Calf woman arrived with the sacred bundle she taught the People of the seven sacred ways to pray. These prayers are through ceremonies that include the Sweat Lodge for purification; the Naming Ceremony for child naming; the Healing Ceremony to restore health to the body, mind and spirit; the adoption ceremony for making of relatives; the marriage ceremony for uniting male and female; the Vision Quest for communing with the Creator for direction and answers to one's life; and the Sundance Ceremony to pray for the well—being of all the People.

EXT. NEW YORK CITY, INTERSECTION OF BROADWAY AND DYKEMAN STREETS

A neighborhood at the top of Manhattan. Predominantly immigrants from the Dominican Republic but also Jews, African Americans and young singers and actors who can't afford to live further downtown.

We cross the street away from the street from the tenements and bodegas and see a children's park, then follow a path that leads up a small mountain, by city standards. A lovely hike with stone steps and benches in places. Near the top are beautiful flower gardens and at the top is THE CLOISTERS, a monastic style group of buildings filled with medieval art.

At the entrance to the Cloisters is a relief of Christ and the two thieves on crosses. There is an inscription in Latin and a supertitle translates it:

> "Through the Sign of the Holy Cross, from our enemies, our God frees us."

EXT. THE PARK NEARBY THE CLOISTERS

In the flower gardens overlooking the Hudson River, Darien stands at an easel and paints. Lakota basks in the sparkling sunlight.

We notice that the landscape of this place strongly resembles the paintings in Darien's studio at the beginning of the story. This is a place that has lived in her unconscious.

A Dominican boy, MANUELITO, five or six years old, runs in the flowers. His sister, ROSA, fourteen, chases him. He stops when he sees Darien. He looks at her canvas. His smile is as brilliant as the sunshine, but his lips are tinged with blue and there are dark circles under his eyes. He looks at the canvas.

MANUELITO

Que cosa?

But his sister has caught him.

ROSA

Manuelito, you mustn't bother people you don't know.

Darien smiles. Manuelito runs over to Lakota and pets her.

DARIEN

It's okay. Now we know each other.

Rosa looks at Darien uncertainly.

ROSA

My brother has a *corazon grande*.

Darien does not understand what Rosa means by "large heart". So Rosa puts her hand over her own heart.

ROSA (CONT'D)

His heart is bad.

Manuelito and Lakota are having a fine time. He yells to his sister.

MANUELITO

Look, *Rosa*, I have a new friend!

Rosa laughs.

ROSA

Come on, sweetheart, *mami* is waiting for us to come to lunch.

Manuelito gets up and dusts himself off. He smiles up at Darien. Then he throws his arms around her and hugs her tightly.

ROSA (CONT'D)

Manuelito—

But the hug is so sweet, Rosa cannot complain any further. Manuelito extricates himself and begins to run down the hill.

ROSA (CONT'D)

Manuelito, wait for me!

Darien watches the two children as they disappear. Lakota is now by her side. She looks at Darien intently and whines a little bit.

DARIEN

What, are you hungry, too?

Lakota continues to whine, but she is also wagging her tail. Then she barks at Darien.

DARIEN (CONT'D)

What is it, Lakota?

Lakota barks again, she is very excited about something.

DARIEN (CONT'D)

Yes, it is a beautiful day, a wonderfully beautiful—

CUT TO:

A FEW MOMENTS LATER

Darien and Lakota follow the wooded trail down to Broadway, the sunshine filters through the trees, a magical sight.

INT./EXT. DYKEMAN STREET

A small market. On the street in front of the store are piles of fresh tropical fruits. Darien selects several pieces of fruit and goes inside with Lakota.

The store owner, RAFAEL, smiles when he sees them, showing the few teeth he still has. Lakota looks at him with interest.

Rafael cuts a big slice of meat and gives it to Lakota. This has happened many times before. He turns to Darien.

RAFAEL

What would you like today, *mi amore*?

Darien puts the bag on the counter.

                    DARIEN
        Just this, I think.

An elderly SENORA stands next to Darien. She watches her closely.

                    RAFAEL
        You paint today?

                    DARIEN
        I paint every day.

                    SENORA
    Rafael, tiene los ojos caliente.

Rafael looks at Darien's eyes.

                    DARIEN
        What did she say?

Rafael hesitates.

                    RAFAEL
        She says you have beautiful eyes.

Darien looks at the Senora.

                    DARIEN
        Oh. *Muchas gracias.*

The Senora runs out of the store. Darien is stunned.

DARIEN

What, what did I do?

Rafael adds some extra fruit and another piece of meat to Darien's bag.

RAFAEL

She is superstitious old fool,that is all. It is your eyes, they are, how do you say, hot. Glowing.

Rafael rings up the amount on an old cash register. Darien gives him some money and picks up the bag. She smiles at Lakota.

DARIEN

If I'm going to live here, I had better learn Spanish, I guess.

She smiles and leaves the store. Rafael watches her go. He exhales a large breath.

RAFAEL

Madre de Dios.

FADE OUT.

INT/EXT. DARIEN'S APARTMENT BUILDING

Music continues to play as we see Darien's home for the first time, a tenement built in the 1950s, concrete and stark outside, but with touches of brilliant colored mosaic tile in the lobby.

Darien and Lakota go into the building and walk up three flights of stairs and go into their apartment. We see her modest furniture but also her PAINTINGS on the walls, landscapes of the park and the Cloisters, and dominating one wall, the IMAGE OF A BLACK WINGED HORSE and the BEAUTIFUL WOMAN who rides her. They are soaring through a brilliant night sky.

Lakota settles down on her bed. Darien goes to her easel and begins to draw the image of a BLACK LABRADOR.

EXT. THE PARK—DAY

Darien and Lakota sit in the sun on a BENCH. Children play in the playground. Their mothers or nannies sit nearby and gossip.

A SMALL CHILD and HIS MOTHER walk by Lakota. The child stops to pet her. Then MANY CHILDREN come. Lakota is the center of attention and she loves it. But always she looks to Darien. Their connection never breaks.

Suddenly PHILLIP appears. The children instinctively move away and return to the playground.

PHILLIP

Can we walk?

CUT TO:

EXT. MAIN STREET—VARIOUS SCENES

Phillip, Darien and Lakota walk along the street. Life and noise are abundant, cars, SENORAS and SENORITAS shopping, VENDORS on the street, mounds of fruit stands,

OLD MEN playing dominos . . .

As they walk, it is clear that Darien is known. People nod and say hello. As they pass her they look uncertainly at the Son.

> PHILLIP
>
> It's good to see you.

He holds her elbow as they walk. A familiar but unearned gesture.

> PHILLIP (CONT'D)
>
> The family is good. Max will go to kindergarten in the fall. My wife is having another baby. It's difficult; she has to rest a lot of the time.

An OLD MAN calls to Darien from his shop window.

> OLD MAN
>
> Darien, *quieres café con leche*?

Darien looks at Phillip.

> DARIEN
>
> Coffee?

CUT TO:

A CAFE TABLE ON THE STREET

Darien and Phillip drink coffee. The Old Man serves Lakota a bowl of milk.

                    DARIEN
          Max is how old now?

                    PHILLIP
          Six. He's behind a year.

                    DARIEN
          Yes, the operation. But he's better?

Phillip smiles brightly.

                    PHILLIP
          Yes, yes, fine. He's fine.

But the smile seems to hurt his face.

                    PHILLIP (CONT'D)
          I feel badly about how . . . Look, my father and I had a difficult
          relationship. It happens, right? Father and son. And now, well,
          it's like, I can't explain it, it's like an emptiness.

Darien reaches out for Lakota and Lakota instantly is at her side.

PHILLIP (CONT'D)

I guess I just wanted to say that to you, I don't want you to think I don't, didn't care, I do, I care very much and I hope, I just hope that at some level he knew. Now I have a son of my own and I can see him looking at me and I haven't even done anything yet, I haven't even given him a reason—

DARIEN

Are you looking for my forgiveness?

Phillip is surprised.

PHILLIP

I'm just trying to say something, for God's sake.

DARIEN

You want me to feel sorry for you, well, I don't. You cannot come and see me to expiate the years you held your father hostage with your anger. It was a long road here and it is a long road back.

Phillip looks down at the ground then gains his courage and speaks.

PHILLIP

When I canceled the policy and took most of your money away, I was just getting back at my father. I've now set up a trust fund for you that will provide amply for you and Lakota for the rest of your lives.

He hands Darien an envelope and stands up abruptly.

PHILLIP (CONT'D)

You can't go back, can you?

Darien looks up at him in the sparkling sunshine.

FADE OUT.

EXT. DARIEN'S APARTMENT BUILDING—YEARS LATER—MORNING

Some years have gone by and it shows in Darien's beautiful face. It is winter. Snow falls lightly as Darien and Lakota finish packing her car.

EXT. MAIN HIGHWAY

Darien and Lakota are driving south. Mist rises from the river below. The shoreline of New Jersey looms in the distance.

CUT TO:

INT./EXT. A SERIES OF SCENES

Darien and Lakota are travelling south. As they drive we see what they see:

Interstate 87 South, the cars drive slowly in the traffic. A FAMILY OF EASTERN EUROPEANS is next to Darien and Lakota. There are more people than seat belts. Suddenly a DOG'S FACE appears in the window, a male Black Lab. He and Lakota look at each other. The family smiles.

Pennsylvania countryside, the Amish in their horse driven wagons. One AMISH YOUTH holds a rope and rollerblades along. Lakota is very interested in this sight. She barks excitedly. The Amish boy sees her and tips his hat and laughs.

Late afternoon, Darien and Lakota have checked into a motel. Darien opens the door and Lakota leaps into the air and lands on the bed.

INT./EXT. A RESTAURANT—THAT EVENING

Outside in the parking lot, we notice that the cars have Virginia plates. Darien and Lakota go inside.

The HOSTESS, a bleached blonde woman with a kind face, greets them.

                    HOSTESS
        May I help y'all?

                    DARIEN
        Table for two.

The Hostess looks around the dining room. Only a few diners tonight. She looks at Lakota.

                    HOSTESS
        Oh, what the hay.

She leads them to a table.

123

HOSTESS (CONT'D)

You here on vacation?

DARIEN

We wanted to go to the beach.

HOSTESS

Bit cold for that.

A SMALL GIRL from another table has run over to pet Lakota. Her MOTHER cautions her.

MOTHER

Ask first!

The girl looks at Darien.

GIRL

Can I pet her?

But the girl has already begun.

GIRL (CONT'D)

What's her name?

DARIEN

Lakota. It means friend.

The Hostess has taken out an order pad.

HOSTESS
Well, Friend. The special is meat loaf.

The girl whispers in Lakota's ear.

GIRL
Don't eat it, it's terrible.

The girl puts her face in Lakota's neck and hugs her tight.

FADE TO:

EXT. VIRGINIA BEACH—MORNING

Darien and Lakota on the beach. It is cold but bright and sunny. Darien is wrapped in a colorful shawl. The wind is against her face. Lakota runs along the water's edge.

Darien sees a Frisbee in the sand and picks it up. She throws it to Lakota and Lakota catches it.

Now they both run as the waves crash at the shore.

CUT TO:

LATER

Darien and Lakota sit on an Indian blanket and eat a picnic lunch together, bread and cheese and fruit. Darien opens cherries and removes the pits and gives several slices of roast beef to Lakota.

Now a MAN approaches them. He is about Darien's age, handsome with dark skin and piercing blue eyes. He could be Indian, he could be Italian or perhaps he is from somewhere that cannot be named.

MAN

Excuse me, I couldn't help noticing your dog.

DARIEN

Yes?

Lakota looks at him. There is something, some kind of recognition.

MAN

I know there are a million Black labs in the world . . .

DARIEN

Not like Lakota.

MAN

Yes.

He kneels down in front of Lakota. She immediately befriends him.

MAN (CONT'D)

When I was young I had a dog. I found her, she was half starved. I brought her home but my parents wouldn't let me keep her.

He looks up at Darien.

MAN (CONT'D)

Isn't that silly? All those years ago but I remember it like it was yesterday. We took her to a pound, but she ran away when I opened the car door. I have looked for her ever since. Of course, she can't possibly be alive.

DARIEN

Perhaps Lakota shares her spirit.

MAN

Is that possible?

Darien laughs deeply but kindly.

DARIEN

Would you like to eat with us?

MAN

I would like that very much.

He sits down.

MAN (CONT'D)

I drive by here almost every day. I have no idea why I stopped.

DARIEN

Really?

Darien hands him some fruit and cheese on a plate.

CUT TO:

EXT. THE HIGHWAY

Darien and Lakota drive again. Her car has the top down and Lakota sits in the front seat with Darien. Lakota wears a red bandana. Rock music plays on the radio. They are having the time of their lives.

EXT. HIKING TRAIL

Darien and Lakota hike on a trail. They pass other HIKERS, families, couples. Everyone stops to pet Lakota. Lakota flushes out some sort of huge bird and speeds after it, quickly returning when she realizes she can not catch it.

LATER

A cold night. Darien sets up a tent for the night. Lakota dozes by the campfire. They hear THE SOUND OF SOMEONE CALLING FOR HELP. Lakota immediately runs in that direction. Darien runs after her.

CUT TO:

ANOTHER CAMPSITE

A family, TWO PARENTS and TWO YOUNG CHILDREN are paralyzed and terrified as A BEAR rummages through their campsite. Lakota runs up to the bear and BARKS WILDLY. The bear ROARS in return.

DARIEN

Lakota!

Lakota continues to BARK. The Bear looks at Darien; a standoff; finally, it quietly turns and walks away.

Darien goes to Lakota.

> DARIEN
>
> It's all right, Lakota.

The Mother grabs her children and takes them inside the tent.

> FATHER
>
> I don't know, I just didn't know . . .

> DARIEN
>
> He won't be back to bother you.

Darien and Lakota turn to go back to their campsite. It is dark and now there are no sounds to guide them. Lakota seems to know the way but Darien trips over a tree root and falls down a long bank.

The Father hears the sounds and grabs a flashlight. He runs toward the SOUND OF LAKOTA BARKING and his flashlight reveals Darien injured next to a large tree.

EXT. MERCY HOSPITAL—LATER

An ambulance pulls up to the hospital. The driver hurries out of the cab and runs around to the back to open the door.

INT. DARIEN'S HOSPITAL ROOM—NEXT DAY

Darien is asleep, but has an IV in her arm. Her chart hangs. from her bed with her name, DARIEN BAER. THE NURSE enters.

Darien opens her eyes.

                    DARIEN

Where's Lakota?

                    NURSE

She's fine—

                    DARIEN

Where is she?

                    NURSE

Sh sh. Freddy the ambulance driver has her. He's a great good, really loves dogs.

                    DARIEN

I want to see her!

                    NURSE

This is a hospital—

                    DARIEN

I want to see Lakota!

Finally the Nurse understands.

CUT TO:

LATER

Darien sleeps in her hospital bed. Then we see Lakota curled up in a chair.

EXT. REHABILITATION CENTER—A WEEK LATER

Darien and Lakota are getting out of an ambulance in front of the Rehab Center. TWO ATTENDANTS come out and help her into a wheelchair. Then one puts a leash on Lakota. Darien speaks to him and he takes the leash off.

We hear a VOICE OVER as they go into the building.

> MAN (V.O.)
> When The Buffalo Calf Woman was done teaching all our people, she left the way she came. She went out of the circle, and as she was leaving she turned and told our people that she would return one day for the sacred bundle. And she left the sacred bundle, which we still have to this very day.

INT. DARIEN'S ROOM

A dreary, institutional room. Four walls, a bed, dresser and a few personal effects.

Darien dozes in her bed. A WALKER is against a wall. DR. GRAHAM enters, a young woman in her early thirties with dark intense eyes. She picks up Darien's wrist and takes her pulse. Lakota sits in a chair and watches the doctor intensely.

                    DR. GRAHAM
          Hey, sleepyhead.

                    DARIEN
          Where is—

But then Darien sees Lakota.

                    DR. GRAHAM
          How are you feeling?

                    DARIEN
          Terrible.

Dr. Graham smiles.

                    DR. GRAHAM
          It'll get better. In a few days we'll have you walking all over the
          place.

She looks at Lakota.

                    DR. GRAHAM (CONT'D)
          I heard you have a roommate.

Dr. Graham goes over to Lakota and pets her. She bends down to Lakota's level. Then she looks out the window. ANOTHER PATIENT is walking a COCKER SPANIEL.

DR. GRAHAM (CONT'D)
You've started a trend. We're now the first rehab center in the country to accept dogs.

Now Darien looks out the window, too. SEVERAL PATIENTS are fussing over the cocker spaniel.

INT. REHAB CENTER, DARIEN'S QUARTERS—A MONTH LATER

Darien's room is full of her artwork. She has painted scenes from her life, the images of people who have been important to her, plenty of Lakota, the Cloisters, it is a mural honoring the time she has spent on this earth. At the center is a White Buffalo.

VARIOUS HALLWAYS AND QUARTERS

As we move around the Rehab Center, we can see Darien's influence. Peeking inside some of the rooms we see various PATIENTS, elderly or injured, painting pictures. In one hallway, we see a display of art work by patients.

MANY PATIENTS are involved in putting up and admiring their work. The image of Lakota is in most of them.

INT. CAFETERIA

The patients of the Rehab Center are sharing dinner in a large dining room. Outside the windows it is snowing hard. A traffic light blinks yellow near the stone wall with 2 nearby young trees drip with snow.

Lakota is having her meal, also, on the floor next to Darien.

AN ELDERLY GENTLEMAN sitting next to Darien looks at her with adoring eyes as she feeds him his dinner.

> ELDERLY GENTLEMAN
>
> I'm not going to take my sleeping pill tonight. I'm going to call my chauffeur and take you dancing.

Darien laughs. AN ELDERLY WOMAN pokes Darien in the arm.

> ELDERLY WOMAN
>
> I'm saving mine up. Never know when you might need them.

She gives Darien a wink, then smiles through her dentures. Darien looks at her a long moment, then wheels herself away from the table.

THE HALLWAY

Darien wheels down the long corridor; Lakota is at her side, as always. Darien turns a corner and the hallway becomes narrower. Fast approaching is another wheelchair. It's driver is an AMERICAN INDIAN, about sixty, a kind, lined face and eyes that suggest he has lived many

lifetimes. When he speaks we realize he is the voice of the story about the Buffalo Calf Woman. His name is CHAVA.

CHAVA

We have a problem.

They do have a problem. As they tried to pass each other, the wheelchairs become locked.

DARIEN

I'm not in the mood for this. Will you kindly move?

CHAVA

Well, I don't know. What will you give me if I do?

Darien is definitely not in the mood for this, either. A struggle ensues. Finally, the wheelchairs release.

CHAVA (CONT'D)

Women drivers . . .

Darien is up to the challenge.

DARIEN

Careful or I'll sic General Custer on you.

Chava throws his head back and laughs.

CHAVA

I think we won that one.

DARIEN

My name is—

CHAVA

I know.

Lakota looks up at him. Chava reaches down and pets her. They have in instant understanding.

CHAVA (CONT'D)

You must have friends in high places.

We see his kind face very closely now. He winks at Darien.

INT. DARIEN'S ROOM—NIGHT

Darien is asleep in her bed. Lakota is wide awake and watching. The mural comes to life. We go inside.

What we see next is Darien's dream. Her face as she sleeps is a ghostlike vision over the scene of a SUN DANCE RITUAL.

As the Ritual comes to life, DARIEN'S FACE disappears. Instead she is part of the dance. Chava is there—Mato Chante.

We see a MAN DRUMMING. He is young and strong and beautiful. We watch him for a few long moments.

The scene changes. We are on the landscape of North Dakota. We still HEAR THE SOUND of the drumming and chanting but Darien is alone. She is dressed as THE WHITE BUFFALO WOMAN.

Darien has a bundle. She lays the bundle down. Darien cries and runs away. We see the bundle. Inside we see the face of a BABY GIRL.

The dreams ends. Darien sits up in bed suddenly, still crying. CHAVA is now sitting next to her bedside. Darien sees him.

> DARIEN
>
> I have a daughter.

> CHAVA
>
> Yes, yes.

> DARIEN
>
> I don't know where she is.

Chava nods and closes his eyes. They remain together in the darkness.

We move away from them to the mural on the wall. THE IMAGE OF A LITTLE GIRL is animated. She looks at Darien.

INT. FRONT DESK

Chava talks to the Front Desk NURSE.

> CHAVA
>
> So why don't I get to have a dog? Darien has a dog.

The Nurse has been on this job for thirty years. She doesn't even look up.

NURSE

Miss Darien pays for that big room. You don't have any money.

CHAVA

Hm. Always money. Where would we be without money?

Chava's wheelchair is suddenly spun around. He looks to see his ROOMMATE, a tall thin man with thick glasses.

ROOMMATE

You ready?

As the Roommate wheels Chava away . . .

NURSE

You boys stay out of trouble, you hear?

She smiles as they wheel down the hallway then goes back to her work.

CHAVA

Darien and Lakota, they are to be respected, do you understand?

The Roommate whistles a familiar tune.

INT. COMMUNITY ROOM—LATER

SEVERAL PATIENTS including Darien are finishing the stitching on their medicine bags. She reaches over and picks up a few beads that Chava has handled. She puts them in her bag.

An Elderly Woman looks out the window.

CUT TO:

INT./EXT. WINDOW TO THE YARD

ELDERLY WOMAN
What do you know, a skunk! And it's near winter. I'll be.

Sure enough there is a skunk. As it travels lazily across the snow covered grass, we notice three babies trailing behind her.

BACK TO:

THE TABLE

They watch in wonder.

EXT. REHAB CENTER GROUNDS—DAY

Darien walks with the use of a cane. She wears her medicine bag now at all times.

Lakota walks with her. Lakota is now walking with great difficulty.

We see that the Center has a wall around the perimeter of the grounds. The wall is made of large stones cemented together. It looks ominous and impenetrable—no one will pass beyond that wall.

A YELLOW BLINKING TRAFFIC LIGHT on the street draws the eye to two trees and a path at one edge. A locked gate and the uncompromising stone wall. Darien looks at the trees and the path. She coughs a little bit. She turns and looks at the Center. In the window she can see Chava watching her.

A feather floats in the air. Darien captures it. She puts it in her medicine bag. An AFRICAN AMERICAN ORDERLY runs across the grass toward Darien.

> ORDERLY

Hey, Mrs. Baer?

Darien turns to look at him.

> ORDERLY (CONT'D)

You got a visitor.

INT. REHAB CENTER MAIN OFFICE

Darien, using a cane, and Lakota follow the Orderly down a hallway to a closed door. The Orderly opens it.

We see a BEAUTIFUL WOMAN around forty. Her long dark hair is plaited in the back. She has Darien's eyes.

> WOMAN

I'm Camille.

Darien searches the woman's face for a moment.

DARIEN

You look like your great grandmother.

Darien puts her cane aside and opens her arms. Camille walks into her embrace. The Orderly closes the door.

EXT. REHAB CENTER GROUNDS—JUST BEFORE SUNSET

Darien, Camille and Lakota are sitting on a blanket on the grass. It is cold. Although the sun still shines, Darien and Camille can see their breath when they speak.

DARIEN   .

My grandmother had just died. I wanted to keep you. The elders in the church . . .

Darien puts her hand to her throat instinctively. She is remembering the Cameo necklace.

DARIEN (CONT'D)

My own mother, your grandmother was very religious. After they took you I left home.

Darien is quiet now. The two watch the sun setting.

DARIEN (O.C.) (CONT'D)

I went to New York. The worst place I could think of. But I liked it. I got a job in a restaurant. That's where I met Edgar.

Darien looks at Camille now.

159

CAMILLE

And my father?

Camille searches her mother's face but cannot read her expression.

CAMILLE (CONT'D)

Were you—?

DARIEN

Oh, no. That wouldn't be possible.

Darien turns a little to look at the building. CHAVA watches her from a window. We see him more closely. Lakota is next to him. We hear CHAVA HUM AN ANCIENT TUNE. We continue to see him as Darien speaks.

DARIEN (O.C.) (CONT'D)

Now that you're here with me, I can't remember when you weren't.

Darien smiles at Camille.

DARIEN (CONT'D)

Do you know what I mean?

Camille looks at the window now then back to her mother.

CAMILLE

I think I do.

Camille looks at Darien's necklace.

                    CAMILLE
        That's beautiful.

                    DARIEN
        It was my grandmother's.

She smiles.

                    DARIEN (CONT'D)
        Like I said, your great grandmother.

Their faces glow from the setting sun. We hear CHAVA SINGING. The SOUND grows stronger and stronger as the scene . . .

                                        FADES OUT.

EXT. REHAB CENTER—LATER

Darien and Camille are saying goodbye. They are hugging, both women are crying. Lakota and CHAVA are behind them.

Camille leans down and pets Lakota.

                    CAMILLE
        You keep her safe for me, okay? I'll be back next month for you.

Camille kisses Chava on the cheek.

CAMILLE (CONT'D)

You get better now, do you hear?

CHAVA

It is done.

Camille turns back to her mother.

CAMILLE

I have a room in the back of the house. It faces east so the sun will wake you every morning.

DARIEN

That will be wonderful.

They kiss one more time. Camille gets into her car, A MUSTANG. She drives away. CHAVA and Darien watch as she disappears.

DARIEN (CONT'D)

Did that really happen?

Chava laughs.

CHAVA

There is only this moment. Whatever you are feeling, that is real. All the rest is an illusion.

DARIEN

Sometimes you don't make any sense.

CHAVA

It's simple. If the past is an illusion and the future is unwritten, why . . .

We see deeply into Chava's eyes now.

CHAVA (CONT'D)

You can create any present moment you want.

EXT. REHAB CENTER GROUNDS—A FEW WEEKS LATER

Darien, still with her cane, walks with Lakota. Lakota is now in a lot of pain but would never leave Darien's side. We see Darien's face. It is ruddy with the cold air. She coughs a little, and then she coughs a little more.

The Orderly runs up to her.

ORDERLY

Miss Darien, you're catching your death.

Darien looks at him.

DARIEN

Am I?

Then she smiles.

DARIEN (CONT'D)

I guess if you can catch your dreams you can catch your death.

ORDERLY

Huh?

Darien coughs more violently. Here

INT. DOCTOR'S OFFICE—LATER

Dr. Graham listens to Darien's lungs. She puts away her stethoscope.

DR. GRAHAM

Pneumonia.

Dr. Graham gives Darien a stern look.

DR. GRAHAM (CONT'D)

Your hip has never healed properly, you're always gallivanting about.

Darien coughs a bit apologetically. Dr. Graham looks at Lakota now.

DR. GRAHAM (CONT'D)

And same goes for you.

Dr. Graham looks at both of them with affection. But there is something else in her eyes. She is seeing two very special creatures whose time in this dimension is coming to a close. Snow falls.

INT. COMMON ROOM—A FEW DAYS LATER

Darien and Lakota are bundled up with an Indian blanket in her wheelchair. They are looking out the window at the yard. It has snowed

several inches. The sky is steel gray and a wind moves through the trees in the distance.

Also in the distance is the yellow blinking light near the edge of the property. Darien's eye lingers there. She pets Lakota who is very weak. Her eyes now have cataracts.

Occasionally, Darien coughs. The Orderly comes up to Darien and touches her gently on the shoulder.

> ORDERLY
>
> You should be in bed. How did you get out here?

> DARIEN
>
> Sing something for me.

> ORDERLY
>
> What?

> DARIEN
>
> Please.

He is embarrassed but wants to please her.

> ORDERLY
>
> I'm not much of a singer.

> DARIEN
>
> *Blue Moon*, do you know that one?

ORDERLY

Should I?

Through the glass in the door we can see the glow of the YELLOW BLINKING LIGHT. He takes hold of Darien's wheelchair.

ORDERLY (CONT'D)
Come on. Let's get you back to your room.

As he wheels her away, we see a lone Lakota warrior in the yard, the same YOUNG MAN we saw in her vision.

As she is helped into bed by putting her arms over the Orderly's neck she deftly takes a pair of scissors and cuts the cord holding the plastic key that opens the back door. Darien holds on to the key unnoticed.

INT./EXT. REHAB CENTER—VARIOUS SCENES

We are seeing the exterior of the building one last time. Then we go inside. The Rehab Center is quiet. We go up and down the hallways and revisit the artwork that the patients have made, the dining room that is set up for breakfast in the morning.

CUT TO:

DARIEN'S ROOM

A CLOCK on her dresser says 1 AM. She crushes white pills in a small bowl. Lakota watches her. She puts the powder in an envelope. Then she takes off the red bandana from around Lakota's neck and replaces it with a BLACK BANDANA.

DARIEN

We will face this together.

She sprinkles half of the white powder in a bowl of meat for Lakota. Lakota eats it. Then she puts the rest in a glass of water and drinks the bitter potion.

We notice an envelope addressed in Darien's handwriting that is propped up on the dresser. It is addressed to Detective O'Connor. Darien touches it.

DARIEN (CONT'D)

I told you one day you would know.

Then she buries her face in Lakota's coat.

INT. DOOR TO GROUNDS

Darien has difficulty getting to the door with Lakota. A large buffalo appears and she supports herself on the animal. She unlocks the door. Darien is becoming dizzy. Lakota cries a little, unable now to help her friend.

CUT TO:

THE GROUNDS

Darien and Lakota are outside. Darien wears her Cameo necklace and she carries a thin hospital blanket. The buffalo disappears into the falling snow.

They walk slowly and steadily to the stone wall and lie down under a small tree in the snow. Darien covers herself and Lakota with the blanket.

The yellow traffic light blinks in the rhythm of Darien and Lakota's heartbeats. Snow falls. They cuddle together and slowly close their eyes.

Time passes; the blinking yellow light turns to red. Five seconds pass and it turns to green. Their journey begins.

THE JOURNEY

Darien is immersed in darkness. A bright white light appears and she slowly moves towards it. Her frail and arthritic body moves across what look like large boulders and through the pain she continues just as she did in life.

CUT TO:

INT. COMMUNITY ROOM—MORNING

Chava sits at a table drinking coffee. Through the window he sees the dead bodies of Lakota and Darien. Tears stream down his cheek.

A NURSE'S AID enters. She is still shrugging off her morning fatigue. She sees Chava.

NURSE'S AIDE

Gawd, my car wouldn't start and it's cold enough to freeze your blood. I don't need trouble. I need peace and quiet.

Chava continues to look out the window.

CHAVA

I think your troubles are just starting.

The Nurse's Aide looks at CHAVA quizzically. Then she follows his line of sight.

> NURSE'S AIDE
> Lord almighty.

CUT TO:

> DARIEN
> She continues to struggle over boulders and jagged pieces of rock. The path is treacherous and steep. On one side suspended in the air are TABLES OF PEOPLE smoking and drinking. They look at Darien and her plight; they couldn't care less.

CUT TO:

THE FRONT DESK

A NURSE is on the telephone. The Nurse's Aide sits in a chair and cries.

> NURSE
> I'm so sorry to tell you . . . no, no priest, not yet, we just found her . . . will you be coming . . .

CUT TO:

CHAVA'S ROOM

Chava wheels into his room. His ROOMMATE, a younger man who walks with a cane, comes out of the bathroom. He still has shaving cream on his face.

CHAVA

I need your help. I need your help to do a ceremony.

CUT TO:

DARIEN'S ROOM

The Nurse and the Nurse's Aide carefully look through Darien's desk and drawers.

NURSE

A cameo, her daughter wants the cameo necklace . . .

The Nurse's Aide picks up the letter addressed to the detective.

CUT TO:

DARIEN

She is weaker, her hands and knees are bloody. Scenes from her life pass through the air, again suspended on nothing. Edgar, the thugs in the subway, Phillip, memories of Lakota on the beach.

Darien is ready to give up and lay for eternity on the PATH. She turns her head upward.

DARIEN

Please . . . please . . . help me . . .

CUT TO:

THE KITCHEN

Chava and his Roommate are in the kitchen. Chava wears a CEREMONIAL HEADBAND AND VEST.

They fill up containers with sliced roast beef. The Roommate starts to put a piece in his mouth. Chava gives him a look that would stop an oncoming train.

ROOMMATE

Sorry.

CUT TO:

THE FRONT DESK

The Nurse's Aide puts the letter in the outgoing mail box.

NURSE'S AIDE

Go with God.

CUT TO:

THE YARD

Chava and his Roommate are outside. The Roommate wheels Chava toward the wall where Darien and Lakota died.

CHAVA

Kneel down, with one knee on the ground and one pointing toward the sky.

183

The Roommate does what he is told although he does not understand.

Chava places the container of meat on the ground.

                          ROOMMATE
     Won't animals get it?

                          CHAVA
     The spirit of the meat will reach her. That's all that matters.

Chava begins to chant. He closes his eyes and turns his face skyward. The Roommate, unsure, also closes his eyes. After a moment he, too, is transported.

Chava stops and opens his eyes.

                          CHAVA (CONT'D)
     This is now sacred ground. We get out of here fast.

DISSOLVE TO:

                          DARIEN
     She lies on the path as if dead a second time. Her hand finds the bowl of food. She takes it and eats.

                                                    CUT TO:

LAKOTA

She is on another path, also exhausted. And she is also saved by a bowl of food. She eats and she begins to walk toward the white light.

BACK TO:

DARIEN

With every step Darien regains her strength. The white light she has followed slowly transforms to green and it becomes a plateau with beautiful flowers and grass.

BACK TO:

LAKOTA

Her world also becomes greener. As she walks, she, too, becomes stronger.

In the distance she can see another path and there is a place not so far away where they will converge. Lakota hears a sound, low and it rises and it is he SOUND OF VOICES CHEERING.

Strange scenes manifest, fountains of multicolored light like water flowing up and spreading out, seeds dropping on the ground and rapidly growing into trees. Swimming jellyfish, frogs, turtles, monkeys join the scene, then vanish.

Now Lakota sees Darien. The paths have joined.

January 17,2013

DARIEN AND LAKOTA

They run to each other. Darien scoops Lakota up in her arms. They are together again and it is as if they have never been parted.

The SOUND OF VOICES CHEERING is like a concert of happiness. Darien and Lakota transform into pure energy.

They are part of the beautiful pristine scene, the rivers, the fields, the flowers.

Their Energy Forms hover over a SMALL GIRL wearing a white dress. She plays in a pile of mud and scoops two fingers of mud and draws them over her forehead and on both cheeks. She pulls out a GOLDEN WATCH AND CHAIN from the mud. The Girl puts the chain over her head.

> WOMAN'S VOICE (V.O.)
> It's time to come in!

The little girl gets up and runs toward a big house, onto the steps and through the front door.

INT. THE HOUSE

Music plays, FREE AT LAST.

A woman sits at a desk, we only see her from the back. She sorts through many pictures.

We see them more closely. They are photos of the PEOPLE who made this story. THESE ARE THE CREDITS. And when we have seen the last photo.

Darien takes Lakota outside and we see Lakota jumping up for a Frisbee that Darien holds.

FADE TO BLACK.